Rosa

Rosa

초판 1쇄 발행일 2019년 4월 1일

지은이_ 김학진
펴낸이_ 김동명
펴낸곳_ 도서출판 창조와 지식
디자인_ 주식회사 북모아
인쇄처_ 주식회사 북모아

출판등록번호_ 제2018-000027호
주소_ 서울특별시 강북구 덕릉로 144
전화_ 1644-1814
팩스_ 02-2275-8577

ISBN 979-11-6003-134-8   03840

지식의 가치를 창조하는 도서출판 **창조와 지식**
www.mybookmake.com

Rosa

HakJin Kim

Characters

Rosa Miller
Anne Miller
Brian Miller
Linda Stewart (Anne's mother)

Paul Parker
Olivia Parker
Nancy Greene
Helen Greene
Tom Greene
Kevin Greene

Alice Brown (Rosa's best friend)
Roy Bacon (Alice's friend)
Ben (a history teacher)
Nora (Linda's dog)

1

Rosa is running down the stairs out of breath to catch the subway train, but she misses it by a second. Left all alone she gets panicked because she knows that it runs at 20-minute interval. There is no one around at that time, and she needs to make up her mind whether she gets out of there or wait for the next one. For a few seconds she regrets that she didn't join her friends who were in a hurry to go home from the cafeteria where they stopped by for a late night snack. At that point Rosa sees a couple walking down the stairs from the opposite direction. She can feel easy for a moment because they are elderly people.

While glancing sideways at them, Rosa steps

back to the stairs little by little just in case. They look normal, but Rosa can't read their faces in the distance. She just sees them get dressed in blue jeans and white T-shirt. She thinks that they stayed long in a cafe after an outing and hurried to go home but missed the train. By the way, they don't stop after touching the ground, and even come to Rosa at a fast pace. All of a sudden Rosa becomes aware that she should get out. She runs up the stairs to the road and runs hard. They seem to come after her, screaming as if they have something to give her back. That makes Rosa run faster and faster.

Rosa opens her eyes in the morning light hearing her mom call from downstairs. She wonders how she lies down in her bed and all she can remember is that the elderly people in their early sixties chased her.

In the kitchen her father, Brian Miller, dressed in his suit sits at the table for breakfast.

"Good morning, dad! How did I come home?" Rosa asks.

"Don't you remember? You looked so exhausted and your face was all wet. I was worried about you so much," Anne, her mother, says.

"You should call me at the bar for a ride. Don't ever come home alone that late at night. You know, you were so reckless!"

"Sorry, mom. It won't happen again. I promise," Rosa says with a shrug.

Anne nods her head to Rosa. "Are you gonna come home right after school today?"

"I don't know. Why?"

"A repairman is coming to fix the spring door at

five. If you are home early, I'll stop by a grocery store," Anne says. "Oh, I asked your grandma to stay with us while your dad is out of town. She is a guardian angel, you know."

In fact, Linda Stewart, Rosa's grandmother, had worked for the government briefly and then P.E. teacher. Even if she is in her mid sixties, she looks sturdy enough to beat any attacker with a broomstick. She has no fear of humans.

"All right. I'll be home before five," Rosa grins at Anne.

"Thanks. Oh, I told him my son's home, you know," Anne winks at Rosa.

Anne always bears in mind that Rosa is the only child who has no backup except her parents. When she says to strangers about her family, Rosa becomes a son. As a good girl, Rosa understands her mother's nonsense.

After breakfast, Brian walks to the garage. "Rosa. Get on the car. I'll get you to school."

"I'll ride my bike to school, dad. Thanks," Rosa

responds.

"Okay. Take care of your mom while I'm away for just three days," Brian says.

"Don't worry about us. I will keep her safe. And Linda is coming to stay with us. She knocks a stranger down with a single blow, you know."

"Take care of yourself, dad! Bye for now!"
Rosa takes her helmet from the side table flanked by the couch and goes out the front door. She begins to pedal her bike.

When she arrives at the entrance of the school, she finds an elderly woman among a crowd of students in the school yard. At first glance, the woman seems to be nobody, but soon Rosa recognizes that she is that woman whom Rosa saw on the subway platform. Rosa gets shocked feeling her heart pounding, and yet she becomes curious about what brings the woman to the school though she thinks that it is nothing but a coincidence.

Some time later when the class begins, Rosa sees the woman enter the next room.

"Did you see the woman pass by the window?" Rosa asks Alice, a classmate as well as her best friend.

"No, but if you talk about the next room, I think she's a substitute teacher. I heard Ben had to be home for his wife today. So she must be the one for his class," Alice answers.

Rosa tries to forget the woman despite being annoyed by her presence. When school is over and everybody hurries to leave school, Rosa sees the woman again in the school yard. But thankfully, she doesn't seem to know who Rosa is.

Rosa gets home a lot earlier than she was asked in the morning. She parks her bike inside the garage and walks down the driveway to the mailbox. She has rarely done this, but to feel safe she has to check if she's been chased by someone. Rosa sees no one in the street over the mailbox. And she goes back to the garage and closes its shutter. After checking every window, she sits on the couch with her cell phone muted. She looks out the windows which are tinted, so visitors can't see inside. Her meticulous mother spent some money for every windowpane in the house to be tinted. Now Rosa feels relieved from psychological threat.

At five o'clock the doorbell rings. Rosa approaches the front door without any noise and peeps through a wide-angle lens on the door. She sees a man who says his name. She almost grabs the doorknob. But she scans the man for a second because he looks a little familiar to her. Suddenly, she finds out that he is the man of last night. At once she covers her mouth with her hands to keep herself from hiccups that occur when she gets chills. She stays put with her cell phone off and keeps watching him through the lens. She sees that he takes out his cell phone after pressing the bell once more.

"Hello, this is Paul Parker from PP Hardware. I think no one is home," he says.

"Oh, I'm so sorry. My son should be home. Do you

mind if you wait for me? I'll be home in ten minutes. Or do you want to set the date for your next visit? Again I'm so sorry," Anne answers.

"I'll wait," he says.

As Rosa hears their conversations, she seems to be frozen on the spot. But she tries to convince herself that he would not remember Rosa as long as she doesn't talk to him first. She takes a deep breath and says to herself that she should not think about her running away from the subway station. Nonetheless, she doesn't open the front door thinking of her mother's frowning face. After hearing Anne lift the shutter of the garage, Rosa goes upstairs to her room and locks the door.

When Rosa wakes up from a short nap, it's almost six o'clock. Feeling the house is strangely quiet, she slips out of the room and tiptoes downstairs. She wonders where her mother is around since there is no noise at all. Fixing the back door seems to be done. She walks to the kitchen to check if Paul of PP Hardware is still there. Anne is not home, and Paul isn't either. She flops down into a chair in the kitchen and then texts Anne.

"Mom, where are you?" she texts.

Anne texts back, "Isn't Linda there yet? She's supposed to get home before six. I'm in the bakery. Do you want to have spaghetti for dinner?"

At that point Rosa hears a knock on the spring door which was fixed an hour ago. Rosa rises to her feet to open it and Linda stands there giving a sweet smile which makes Rosa feel great tenderness for her. As soon as Linda gets inside, she takes stuff out of her bag.

"Ta da! Here's your spring jacket! I knitted it," Linda says.

"Oh, thanks, grandma. It's awesome that you're knitting," Rosa grins.

At once Rosa puts it on and walks forward like a fashion model with her hands at her sides. Linda looks happy with her granddaughter.

"Hmm, it suits you fine. My fashion sense is good," Linda says.

"Grandma, you are perfect. I love you," Rosa hugs Linda.

Since Linda lives a ten-minute drive from Rosa, they meet as often as time allows and share almost everything.

As the night goes on, all three women feel good after dinner and sit together on the sofa to watch local TV news. While they listen to the issue of missing children, Rosa mindlessly brings up her running away from strangers. On seeing Anne's eyes widened in curiosity, Rosa turns aside from it and asks, "By the way, did you know the repairman?"

"No, I just found his shop from the internet. He runs a big hardware store," Anne answers. "So, what you're saying is someone ran after you last night, huh?"

"No, I didn't say that. I was just talking about the news," Rosa says nonchalantly.

She thinks that she should keep her mouth shut until she can be sure to tell them about the elderly couple.

2

The next morning Rosa looks up at the sky that is overcast with dark clouds. It looks like rain at any moment. Rosa puts her swimsuit in her backpack instead of a tennis racket. Linda already starts the engine with her remote control as she leaves the kitchen door and calls out Rosa loudly. Rosa sits in the passenger seat and says, "I didn't ask you for a ride to school."

"As long as I stay in your house, giving you a ride is my job. Besides, today it's going to rain hard," Linda says.

"When are you going to get your driver's license?"

"Soon, grandma, I love your car," Rosa answers.

"The old lady like me has to drive a big car. I know I don't look old, but I can't ignore my age," Linda shrugs her shoulders.

Rosa laughs and says, "You still look like a fifty-year-old woman. I mean it."

Before they arrive at the school, rolls of thunder are heard in the distance and then it begins to rain.

As Rosa runs to the building, she finds Alice ahead of her. They both hold their backpack above their heads. At the gate Alice says to Rosa, "We can't play tennis after class. Let's go swimming."

"Sounds good," Rosa says.

As soon as school is over, Rosa leaves the classroom to meet Alice before going to the swimming pool together. In the hallway, Rosa finds an old man who is standing with his back to her. At once she recognizes him as Paul because of his cap which she has seen before. She slips by him quietly because she doesn't want to catch his eyes. By the time she hears nothing from behind, she sees Roy, her classmate, coming to her. But he walks straight past Rosa and says, "Hi, Mr. Parker. Are you still working on the door? It seems to take a long time in your hands."

Rosa is stunned when she hears Roy say so. She says to herself, "What? Does Roy know him? Oh my! What the hack is going on? He is my neighbor, huh. Then the elderly people who ran after me were Paul and Olivia. They were not as scary as I thought. I didn't have to run away from them. But to me they looked like taking me away. I don't know why I misunderstood them like that though they won't do harm to me. Well, everything's clear. He's just an ordinary neighbor who Roy talks to in a friendly way. Oh, I feel relieved."

That afternoon Rosa enjoys swimming with Alice, and then two girls walk to the shopping mall which is ten minutes from the school. Since Rosa and Alice have known each other for a long time, they have no secrets from each other. Once they get to talking, they have to go on for hours. As they sit at the table after ordering two slices of pizza and sodas, Rosa brings up the incident she hasn't told Alice yet.

"You know, we and other girls went to the bar the day before yesterday," she says to Alice.

"Yeah, did you see anyone like Roy in the bar?" Alice asks.

"No! I left the bar ten minutes after you guys, but I missed the subway in a second. I was scared of being all alone, and thanks to the Lord, I saw an elderly couple coming down the stairs. But that was wrong. They came straight to me, so I began to run up the stairs to the road. When I looked back I found they were chasing me, so I ran hard. I made it to my house though I didn't remember it," Rosa says.

"That's it? Rosa, your running isn't a secret," Alice says in an indifferent tone.

"That's not the end. I found out the elderly couple were Paul and a substitute teacher. Isn't it a surprise?" Rosa says.

"You mean Paul and a substitute teacher, Olivia?"

Alice asks.

"Yeah, do you know Paul, PP Hardware store?" Rosa asks.

"Yeah. I think Roy's home is on the same street as Paul's house. By the way why did you think they ran after you? That's odd, huh," Alice says with a puzzled look.

Rosa shrugs her shoulders to Alice and says, "I don't know, but I'm sure they chased me. Since that night I met them by a curious coincidence. I saw Olivia at school and Paul through the wide-angled lens of the front door. So I've taken them for mysterious people who tried to take me away. Well, but now I feel better after I saw Roy say hello to Paul. And you tell me where they live, so the encounter of that night was nothing but a happening."

"I understand. If they were not Roy's neighbors, they would be real strangers like you thought," Alice says

While listening to Alice, Rosa stays silent and thinks

that she would never do something that would judge others hastily though she doubts the elderly couple's sudden appearance was odd.

3

Next morning everything looks good to Rosa. A new day starts as usual and her heart feels much lighter now. In the morning sunlight, Rosa gets on her bike and looks around and then starts pedaling. The cool breeze gently touches her face and one of torn flower petals blown in the breeze falls on her head. As she tries to catch it, she sees a metal gray van with its store name--PP Hardware--parked at the corner of the street. The presence of Paul's van frightens her a bit, but this time she intends to ignore it assuming that one of her neighbors may call to have things fixed.

Meantime in the kitchen where Anne and Rosa left a mess, Linda sits alone at the table reading a morning newspaper. After a half hour, she rises to her feet to get ready to take a walk with her dog which has never been apart from her since its adoption. The dog on a leash is trotting along at her side, soon sniffs here and there and gets ahead. Linda and the dog take a round to the park nearby. On the way back home Linda finds the van at the corner which Rosa saw while going to school. No sooner has Linda got near to the van than the driver's door swings open and there Paul shows up. Paul blocks her path and speaks to Linda.

"Oh, I'm sorry. I didn't know you were coming. Forgive me if I freaked you out," Paul says.

"That's okay. I should be careful. It's my fault that I got close to the van," Linda says.

Linda talks to Paul who is oddly familiar to her, and tries to pretend to run into a neighbor in her smile.

"Oh, you are from PP Hardware. I often go to the store to find stuff for my garden. You are busy with your job, huh," Linda says.

Paul stares at Linda and says, "Yep. By the way I'm

Paul Parker. This may sound odd, but I think I saw you somewhere a long time ago."

"Mr. Parker, I don't think so. I moved in from the west a few years ago. Well, I need to go on walking. Have a nice day. Bye," Linda responds and takes off at once.

Linda turns her back on Paul hoping that he couldn't recognize her. Feeling her heart pounding due to shock, she walks back to the park with her dog instead of going Anne's home. She has never imagined that she would encounter Paul in the street of her neighborhood. She mutters to herself, "How can he show up like this? Definitely he knows me. That's why he said he had met me. Oh, he's driving me nuts."

Paul's sudden presence pushes Linda to recall that day seventeen years ago. Looking back on the day Rosa was born, Linda still doesn't know what she was supposed to do. To tell the truth, Linda didn't do wrong at all; she was just in the wrong place at the wrong time.

She just saw a nurse who was working in the hospital's newborn unit at the time of two babies' births, and a man who entered the room in which visitors could watch newborns through the window just a few minutes after Linda witnessed something that the nurse made.

As Linda reaches the park, she sits on a bench with her dog on her lap. In a very calm and quiet atmosphere, the recollection comes across her mind. It was a cloudless morning when she got a phone call from her pregnant daughter, Anne. She was told that Anne's labor had started. Hours later, Linda discovered that Anne gave birth through a cesarean section after enduring three hours of labor in the hospital. In the newborn unit Linda had waited to see her granddaughter. At last Linda saw a nurse enter the unit with Anne's baby. By the way Linda happened to find out her granddaughter didn't wear her ID band around her wrist and there was another ID band on the floor which was slipped off a newborn baby who came in a few seconds before. At that point the nurse wrapped Rosa Miller's ID band on the newborn whose band had slipped off to the floor.

Linda was dumbfounded, but she couldn't do anything because it happened too fast for her to fix it and she wasn't sure of telling the nurse which is which; she couldn't be sure she saw it rightly. As a result, Linda had, in a sense, overlooked the nurse's mistake by her silence. In a moment of time the process of wrapping the ID bands was over. Linda was at the scene while two newborns seemed to be switched by the nurse's careless action. She stood still asking herself whether she had to knock the window to let the nurse check which baby is Rosa. Just then, she saw a man--Paul-- come to see his newborn granddaughter. Linda was at a loss thinking what she should do over and over.

Since then Linda has kept her mouth shut about the secret of the ID bands. Rosa has been as precious as gold to Linda as she grew into a lovely brunette with brown eyes though she is relatively short since her infant days unlike her parents, Anne and Brian, who are tall and blond.

As Linda sees a woman pass by them with a dog, she is brought back to reality. She rises from the bench and says to herself, "Nothing's going to happen. Seeing him now before me is absolutely a coincidence."

4

In a warm spring light, Paul stands still leaning against his van after Linda left. He keeps thinking of Linda who looked at him in dismay, which makes Paul convince that he must be known to her. He thinks that Linda might be shocked when she encountered Paul since she has never imagined that she was the one that Paul has searched for in recent years. Then she would wonder how they ran into each other near her daughter's house. Linda's defensive attitude was a disappointment to Paul, but Paul feels satisfied from meeting her.

As for Paul's past life, there was no reason to envy what others had. When Paul became an adult, he was already affluent enough to run several big stores including the PP Hardware store with a large property inherited from his father. But things began to change when his first grandson was born with a kidney failure. As a family man, Paul tried to do his best for his first grandchild and Nancy, his only daughter, dealing with any challenges in keeping his family safe and happy. And he also pushed Nancy to have another child in case she lost her baby boy since he sensed that Kevin Greene, his son-in-law, became estranged from Paul over a money problem and seemed to see another woman; Kevin could leave Nancy if he put his mind to it.

The day came on which Nancy gave birth to a baby girl. Paul headed to the hospital without his wife who had to be with their first one-year-old grandson. He entered the newborn unit which had a big glass window for visitors to watch babies and saw a middle aged woman who already had been looking at two newborn babies. At first glance the woman looked nervous, but Paul, an outgoing man, didn't pay attention to her face and introduced himself. She smiled at Paul telling him her name--Linda--with a bit surprised glance. In a few minutes she left in a hurry and Paul felt sorry not to ask her granddaughter's name as he watched her back walking away. Then, he turned his head to his granddaughter who wore the wrist band named Helen. Helen seemed to look up with a puzzled look. Contrary to his expectations, Helen was blond. She looked so adorable through the window pane. He fixed his gaze at his granddaughter saying "Oh, you are Helen. I'm your grandpa, Paul. What a surprise! You are blond, huh. Our family had scarcely been blond with bright blue eyes. But it's okay with me. You are a pretty girl. I'll meet you soon at home. Bye, now."

Then he went to Nancy who lay flat on the bed in the recovery room, receiving a phone call from Olivia who informed that Paul alone would visit Nancy. He found Nancy look weary after being delivered of a healthy baby girl one year after the first one, but she seemed to feel relieved because she could feel a hope in her second baby.

Since the first one was born with a kidney failure, Nancy had made an effort to have the baby receive treatment with every possible means. Paul knew what was happening in Nancy's mind. She had been clutching at straws while her son had kidney dialysis treatment. After she found out that her immediate family including her didn't have the same blood and tissue types for a kidney transplant, she had to put her son's name on a waiting list until a suitable donor kidney was located. And then she decided to have the second baby as soon as possible for her first son who needed a sibling as Paul suggested.

Looking at Nancy, Paul had been heartbroken, so he supported her with his money and time by trying everything he could do for his daughter. He registered his grandson's name at a special hospital for a future kidney transplant in advance. When Helen was one year old, Paul's grandson went through a kidney transplant and got well enough to spend time with his peers.

Everything around Paul went fine except Nancy who became a divorcee. Helen, a blond toddler, grew up well in a loving family and then Paul could focus on his own life expanding his business.

After looking at his watch Paul gets in the van to leave for his shop and sighs mumbling, "Fate works in a strange way, as the saying goes." Every time he remembers what happened to his family two years ago he can feel his heart freeze. He still shakes his head when it comes to the horrible incident.

It was a terrible car accident that Nancy had. She was injured seriously and her two children were worse. Her son who had grown up as a healthy teen was in critical condition and her daughter, Helen, died at the scene. At the worst news in his whole life Paul collapsed and almost lost the will to live when he heard that his grandson ended up in the hospital. Eventually Paul and Olivia became hospitalized because they couldn't live everyday life in a state of shock. As they knew that Nancy was recovering from her head injury, they got out of the hospital. They had to go through their hardship for Nancy who had been devastated by losing her two kids.

Nancy, being discharged from the hospital, stayed with her parents. She couldn't be free of her mishap, so she stayed up every night though she took pills for depression. Her state of mind seemed to get worse by being treated with more pills. It was heartbroken for Paul to see his loving daughter who never spoke to nor looked at anyone.

In the meantime a very odd thing happened around Paul. One day at his study he found a piece of official paper which was issued by the hospital where Nancy and her two kids had been for a while after the car accident. It read that late Helen's blood type was B. At first Paul passed it, but he began to think about the blood type of Nancy's family. Nancy's blood type was A, and her divorced husband was A, then it was impossible for their children to be type B. It struck Paul that the babies were switched at the hospital whoever did that on purpose or not. He was stunned by the unbelievable truth, but his mind went in a different direction at once thinking of his daughter, Nancy, who had never gone out even for a walk after she lost her two kids. The only way that Paul could do for Nancy seemed to find her own flesh and blood who she wouldn't have thought of.

From that day forward, Paul made a plan to get Nancy her biological daughter and began to find the nurse who was in charge of the newborn unit where his granddaughter was put after birth. Soon he was told from the hospital that the nurse on duty on the day when Nancy gave birth to a baby girl already resigned and there was no mistake done by that nurse. The response given by the hospital official made Paul feel discouraged, but Paul couldn't let it go. He set out in search of his real granddaughter.

The next year Paul found out Linda's location by the

help of a private detective who Paul commissioned. It wasn't hard to know her whereabouts because of a visitors' book of the hospital. According to the information given by the detective, much to his surprise, Linda has lived in Paul's neighborhood. Paul was told that she was a high school teacher in the west but packed up after losing her husband because she couldn't stay alone far from her daughter, Anne. Since then Linda got used to go to Anne to give a hand. Seeing Anne and Rosa everyday has given Linda a sense of purpose to her life.

On hearing of Rosa, Paul was delighted because he knew by intuition that she must be the one that should have been his biological granddaughter. In the same way his late Helen must have been Linda's granddaughter. And he moved on to fix this tough situation.

As everything seemed clear, Paul told Olivia what happened to their family and discussed what to do with her. Like a retired history teacher, Olivia suggested that they clam up until they made it to an amicable settlement. The first thing they had to do was that they would be around Miller's family to collect data about Rosa's schedule that would make things easier for them to contact Rosa. Though they knew that they had no way to be intimate with Rosa, they had to rack their brains to get her stuff like her hair or her tooth brush for a DNA test.

While Olivia started out as a high school substitute teacher of Rosa's school district, Paul registered his hardware store to fix stuff in the high school. They decided not to scare Rosa, their biological granddaughter, any more since that night at the subway station. From then on, Rosa becomes a beacon of hope for them, especially for their ill daughter, Nancy.

5

Linda comes back her home with her dog instead of Anne's. She needs to take a rest to calm down herself after encountering Paul. She also has to think what she can do if Paul asks her to disclose the happening. Though she has done nothing bad to him, his presence causes her to have butterflies in her stomach.

She dials Anne's number and says, "What time are you available today?"

"I'll see you there at 3."

In the cafeteria Linda finds Anne sitting by the window who seems to check cell phone messages. Anne working as a social worker near her house can have a break for a half hour any time.

Anne looks up and says, "Mom. why here? You'll stay with me tonight. Did something come up?"

"The coffee in this café tastes good, you know," Linda smiles.

"I'll have a latte, please. Thanks," Linda says to a waitress.

"Listen, Anne. I'm gonna say things about seventeen years ago when you gave birth to Rosa. It may sound crazy," Linda starts to talk.

Linda takes a deep breath and tells Anne what happened in the newborn unit and about Paul who appeared at the corner of Anne's house around noon.

Anne interrupts Linda. "You mean Paul? PP Hardware store?"

"Maybe. I saw him getting out of that van," Linda responds.

Linda continues with what went on that day and finishes saying that she's been dubious about ID wrist bands that then a nurse worked on by mistake.

Soon, Anne asks, "So, you are sure the babies were

switched or what?"

"I don't know it exactly. I've thought it might happen. I should have called the nurse about the ID band at that moment," Linda says.

"No! It's impossible. Rosa is my daughter. Mom, you should never say that again," Anne shouts with an angry voice.

"Yeah, absolutely," Linda nods.

Thirty minutes later, Anne and Linda rise their feet together. Linda gets in her car to go back to Anne's home and Anne goes back to the office.

Linda glances at her wristwatch to check whether she has time to stop by at the market for some groceries. Preparing dinner for Anne and Rosa is great pleasure to Linda. At the poultry section in the market she picks a pack of fresh chicken breasts and hears the voice of a woman asking how to cook it. At the moment Linda turns her head to the woman to talk back, to her surprise, she sees Paul again. Linda tries to conceal her emotion and says, "After slicing it, place it on the hot grill and cook for two minutes and then broil it with soybean based sauce." And she smiles at Paul.

"We meet twice a day, huh. Now we are casual acquaintances, aren't we?" Paul grins.

"This is my wife, Olivia."

Olivia holds out her hand and says, "Nice to meet you, Ms..."

"Linda Stewart. Nice to meet you, too, Olivia. I'm happy to see such a nice neighbor."

"Oh, by the way, I'd better get going before my granddaughter comes home from school," Linda says promptly.

"Sure. Linda, do you mind if I ask your cell phone number?" Olivia asks with a smile.

They exchange their phone numbers.

On the ride home from the market Linda thinks of Paul's face feeling odd and says to herself, "Something is going on without my knowing." Then she shakes her head. "No no. It can't be. But what if Paul's sudden presence is related with Rosa? I have to use my brain for this." As soon as Linda gets in the kitchen, she calls Rosa to check if she's all right.

"Hi, sweetie, where are you? Are you coming home now?" Linda asks.

"Not yet. I'm in school with Alice. It's early to go home, grandma. By the way, I was gonna ask mom's permission to have a sleepover at Alice's house," Rosa answers.

"Oh. I see. But you can come over here with her," Linda says.

After a little pause Linda hears Rosa's loud voice which resonates through the air in a noisy hall. Then, Rosa says to Linda, "Sorry, grandma. Alice says some other girls will join us."

"Okay, Rosa. Then ask Anne and take care of yourself. Don't be silly all through the night," Linda says.

"All right. Don't worry about me, grandma. I'll see

you tomorrow," Rosa finishes.

Linda puts her cell phone on the kitchen table and washes her hands to start cooking. While chopping onions and celery and sautéing them with other ingredients, she seems to take her mind off Paul.

As Linda finishes making a dish with chicken breasts, she sits on the sofa turning on TV. In a few seconds she sees a message pop up on the screen of her cell phone. She finds that it's from Olivia. It reads, "I'd like to call you now if you can get the phone." Linda ignores it, but soon the cell phone rings. Linda lets the phone keep ringing and doesn't take it to the end.

"Your cell phone is ringing, mom. Oh, you don't take it on purpose. Who's calling?" Anne says to Linda as she enters the living room.

Linda looks up at Anne with tears in her eyes. Since Linda has never been a weak woman as far as Anne knows, Anne thinks there must be something wrong with her.

"Mom, what's happening? Did anything bad happen to you? Are you sick?" Anne asks.

"No. But I don't know why Paul and his wife are hanging around me these days," Linda says.

This time Anne realizes that Paul of the hardware store doesn't appear to Linda for nothing. It is certain that Paul has kept track of Linda to detect what Linda hides. Linda has no idea about since when she has been chased, but when she is conscious of Paul's presence, she seems to be scared and becomes frustrated. Then, Anne comes to think what if Rosa isn't her biological daughter, but soon she shakes her head hard denying the unbelievable happening that she heard from Linda in the afternoon at the café.

Anne and Linda finish their meals in a quiet mood. Since they have no information about Paul, they can't talk about him.

"Anne, I think I need to meet Paul in person because he is likely to talk with me. How about inviting him here tomorrow before Brian returns from his business trip," Linda says.

"Rosa says she'll be home about 6 o'clock. So I'm gonna ask him if he's available at three o'clock."

"Mom, do you want me to join?" Anne asks.

"No. You don't have to," Linda says.

Linda texts to Olivia to arrange a time for their meeting.

6

Linda prepares tea and coffee with some cookies and an apple pie for the guests. About four o'clock Paul and Olivia arrive at the door. Linda greets them with a smile, but there is awkwardness when their eyes meet. As Paul and Olivia sit at the table, Linda brings a coffee pot and a tray of cookies with apple pie.

"I'll have a piece of pie. Hmm, it tastes great," Olivia says.

Both women begin to talk about cooking until being interrupted by Paul.

"Sorry to meddle in. But I think I have to talk about the important issue," Paul starts.

Linda mumbles, "This moment is what I've been

afraid of."

"Linda, I really don't want to offend you, but I've been so curious about what happened to my granddaughter, Helen, seventeen years ago. I already inquired about if the hospital did anything wrong like changing babies by accident. The hospital official denied firmly and eliminated that possibility. So I came to think of you because you were the only one in that unit at the right moment when two newborns entered."

"Well, I don't think you know what blood type your granddaughter is, do you?"

"No, I've never asked Rosa about that," Linda answers plainly.

But she can feel her heart beating. Paul looks at Linda's eyes and continues, "Our Helen's blood type should be A or O, but she was B."

Paul closes his eyes and swallows his saliva to keep him stable. Olivia stays quiet listening to her husband's words.

"Oh! really? When and how did you know Helen's

blood type?" Linda asks.

Paul's mind reels at the question since he's been thinking how he can explain this whole tragic story-- Helen has gone and she was one of the Millers. Some day he should tell the truth which would be unspeakable suffering to Miller's family and Linda. But, this time, Paul makes up his mind to focus on exploring that Rosa is his real granddaughter. On Paul's side, Nancy who lost her two kids including Helen and became mentally ill has been a biggest concern so that he hasn't thought of Linda or Miller's family who will be devastated when they realize that Helen doesn't exist in this world.

"We happened to know her blood type when she was hospitalized since she fell from the stairs of the stadium. Luckily, she gets well," Paul lies.

For some time heavy silence hangs among them and Linda opens her mouth with clenched teeth.

"Well, I don't know what to tell you. If there was something you missed in that room, it would be the ID band which slipped from a newborn baby. And the second baby came in a few seconds later without her ID band around her wrist. The nurse on duty lifted the fallen band and put it on the newborn baby who was expected to have it. But I wasn't sure that she did it right. Now, you are saying that the fallen ID band was put on the wrong newborn baby. I have never doubt it, but now I feel something wrong was done. If that extremely unthinkable incident happened, what should we do?" Linda says with a trembling voice.

They all sigh and silence falls in the room again. At that point Linda's dog swings its tail running to the backdoor. Their eyes pop while finding who comes in. Much to their surprise, there stands Rosa who comes home earlier. All three of them are startled enough to rise to their feet all together. Rosa is just looking at them losing her words.

"Oh, you're early. Mr. and Mrs. Parkers stopped by to have some coffee. Rosa, this is Mrs. Olivia Parker," Linda says.

"Hi. I think I saw you in school when I went to class as a substitute teacher. I'm Olivia and this is Paul," Olivia says to Rosa extending her hand for a handshake.

Rosa also extends her hand, "Nice to meet you, Mrs. Parker."

Rosa smiles at Paul and Olivia as if they look new to her. But soon she excuses herself and goes to the staircase to get out of the dining room.

7

Rosa climbs into her bed and lies flat on her back watching the ceiling blankly. A flood of thoughts pass through her mind. She recalls the faces of the elderly couple at the subway station who chased her yelling something. And this time they showed up and talk a mysterious story with Linda. Before seeing Mr. and Mrs. Parker in the dining room, Rosa almost forgets about them because she happened to know they were normal people. But their presence in front of her makes her feel uncomfortable again. Besides, she hardly believes her ears about what she overheard outside the dining room--blood type and a nurse and the ID band. The more she thinks over, the more she feels complicated. Rosa knows what her blood type is--A. Suddenly, she feels dizzy as a matter of serious concern comes to her mind.

It looks like Rosa needs time to get her thoughts into shape. She feels like throwing up but restrains herself from it. Instead, she takes her cell phone and calls Alice.

"Hey, what's up?" Alice answers.

"Can I see you right now at MacDonald's? I need to talk," Rosa says.

"Come on. Why are you rushing around? I just arrived home a few minutes ago," Alice says.

"Well, I can't hold a huge secret by myself," Rosa says in a weak voice.

"All right. I'll see you there twenty minutes later," Alice surrenders.

Speaking of Alice, she is a real beauty with an outgoing personality but taciturn, so she has never leaked a secret. Though she is popular in school, she is a little picky in choosing friends but likes to spend time with

Rosa who has been good at sports.

Still lying on her bed Rosa pulls herself together thinking what to tell Alice. She figures out that she shouldn't belong to this home; she isn't Anne and Brian's daughter by birth and Linda isn't her grandma. By the time she muses on what she overheard, she hears a knock at the door.

"Sweetie, can I come in?" Linda whispers.

"Yes, grandma, the door's open," Rosa shouts as if she is disrupted.

Linda enters and tries to read Rosa's mind and asks, "What do you want for dinner? There are cookies and pie in the kitchen."

"Grandma, I'm going out to MacDonald's. I'll have a chicken burger with Alice. We have a project to talk about and it won't take long," Rosa says cutely.

As Linda watches Rosa turn the corner of the street, she looks at her own face reflected on the tinted windowpane. She thinks her face is clouded with anxiety. Due to this serious issue, she becomes hollow-cheeked and looks older than she used to do. Since she encountered Paul, she has lost her appetite. She even doesn't sleep well worrying what the future of all is going to be like. Sitting on the couch with another cup of coffee she closes her eyes thinking how she can explain the truth to Rosa who doesn't seem to know what is going on. Still, she can't come up with a good solution.

Inside the MacDonald's a few seats are occupied and Alice comes in a couple of minutes after Rosa. They sit by the window before ordering food.

"Alice, what will you have? I buy you. Don't say no," Rosa insists.

"A cheese burger with a coke," Alice says.
A while later when they are almost done with their meals, Rosa brings up the issue which she has concerned.

"Alice, you know what? Today I saw Mr. Parker and his wife at my home. They were talking with my grandma when I joined them by chance. All three of them looked surprised with my presence. They didn't seem to know that I overheard, so I just said 'hello' to them and went upstairs," Rosa says plainly.

"Really? I wonder why they showed up. Tell me what you overheard," Alice says.

Rosa takes a deep breath

"Alice. This sounds really absurd. Paul has a granddaughter whose name is Helen. Recently he found out Helen's blood type. It was B that couldn't be a supposable case because her parents' blood types are A. I have no idea why he disclosed Helen's blood type. But somehow he is trying to find his real granddaughter," Rosa begins.

"I think my grandma was a witness according to Paul because she had been in the newborn unit before Paul arrived. So Paul insisted that Linda must have seen what happened in the newborn unit though he missed it. And Linda said that the only thing she saw was an ID band on the floor which slipped off from the first baby.

And then the second baby came in without her ID band which wasn't put by the nurse's mistake."

"I think the first baby was meant to be Helen, but the nurse put the ID band 'Rosa' on the first one. I became Rosa instead of Helen. It sounds weird," Rosa finishes.

Alice listens to Rosa without cutting her off in the middle.

"You're supposed to be Helen, huh. Wait a minute! I think I heard that name. Yeah, Helen was always with Roy," Alice says with her eyes wide open.

"Really? I haven't seen her at school," Rosa says feeling a bit jealous of Helen.

"She goes to a private school. You know, her grandpa is rich," Alice shrugs.

"I see. Anyway, if this whole story is really true, tell me what to do," Rosa says.

They both become quiet for a while. Alice slowly rises to her feet and says,

"Rosa, I think you'd better let it go for now and

then sleep well tonight. Let's talk about this tomorrow," Alice says.

On the bike ride home Rosa feels the wind in her hair which is a lot warmer giving the notion that summer is around the corner. From the distance her father's car jumps to her eyes. Wheeling her bike into the garage, she sees Brian alone watching TV in the living room. At the spring door of the kitchen she breathes deeply to behave as usual like she knows nothing about the conversation of Paul and Linda. She enters the kitchen in which the light is on and hears Anne's angry voice.

"Mom. I said it couldn't happen to us. Rosa is my daughter. I don't want to talk about that any more. And I don't believe what Paul said any way," Anne says.

As Rosa hears her mom's voice, she makes a noise by opening and closing the kitchen door on purpose.

"I'm home. Where are you?" Rosa shouts deliberately.

"Oh! Rosa. When did you get in? Did you lock the

garage door?" Anne asks.

"Yep. I did. I'm your daughter. I've never make a mistake twice," Rosa grins to her mom.

"Why are you so nervous to granny? Is there something wrong about me?" Rosa asks with a doubtful look.

"No!" Anne and Linda say at the same time with their eyes popped.

Rosa shrugs and goes to her dad who seems to focus on TV drama.

"Hey, dad, you're home. How was your business trip?"

8

Rosa falls asleep as soon as she lies on the bed as if she has carried big loads. She sleeps deeply until the morning light shines on her face. And then her day starts with anxiety. While riding her bike, she thinks of Paul and Olivia all the way to school. Now that she understands why Paul and Olivia chased her that night, she easily guesses that they have been around her for a certain time period and appeared in front of Rosa to take a chance to pick up any stuff like a few strands of her hair for a DNA test.

Rosa decides that she never speak out what Linda and Paul talked about in the kitchen, but she is very anxious to run away from this situation. She wants to leave her home to some place where any one can't find her. Before the class starts, Rosa texts, "Alice, do you have time after school?"

Alice texts back, "I'll see you at my place."

Alice gets her home first and then Rosa rings the bell after putting her bike in the driveway.

"Come in! Do you want some drink?"
They sit at the kitchen table with some soda. There seems no one in the house.

"Alice, I'm so tired with this situation. What can I do? Can I just wait until everything is settled?" Rosa starts to talk.

"I think Paul will do something like a DNA test by all means. After getting the result he may file a suit against mom and dad to take me. Then Linda won't stay quiet for them to take me from Anne. By the way I wonder if Helen knows her grandfather tries to put his biological one in her place. It's odd. I don't think Helen and her mother let Paul do this if they have lived together for seventeen years caring each other."

"Ah! Can you call Roy to come over here now? I wanna know how Helen is doing these days."

Alice texts to Roy at once and gets a message back from Roy in a minute. Alice says that he'll come to visit them in ten minutes.

"Hey, Alice. Hi, Rosa. Here I am. Any questions?" Roy says getting in the kitchen from the back door.

"It may sound odd, I guess. But are you intimate with Helen?" Rosa asks.

After a little thought, Roy answers, "About eight years since third grader, we've been close friends. Not now. She died in a car accident two years ago."

"What? Helen passed away?" Rosa shouts in a shock.

"Yeah. Nancy, her mother, had a car accident. She was on the way to her summer house with Helen and her brother. Helen died at the scene of the accident and her brother was in critical condition but died a week later. Nancy alone survived but is almost a dead woman now. I don't know exactly how she's doing. I heard she never meets anyone except her psychiatrist. Helen was a tall blonde girl," Roy says in a mood of sadness.

"Oh, I'm so sorry to hear that. How could it happen? I can't believe it," Alice says hastily.

Rosa is quiet at the table. The terrible story about Helen causes Rosa look dumbfounded. Roy looks down at Rosa wondering why she's so shocked by Helen's sudden death. And he pays attention to Rosa for the first time. He has never looked at this brunette girl who is just normal but very athletic.

"Rosa, are you okay? You look pale," Roy asks.

Rosa doesn't look up at Roy and says nothing.

"This is very complicated, huh. Roy, I think you'd better go now. We thank you so much for stop by," Alice says quickly.

Roy grabs the door to leave glancing worriedly at Rosa and gets out of the house.

There is a silence hung in the kitchen for a time.

Though Alice and Rosa have not known Helen, her tragic death brings them to their senses.

"That explains this whole odd happening. The tragic accident almost destroyed Nancy's family. And Paul might find something about Helen like a blood type. With his money he decided to turn him into a grandfather again by finding his biological descendant who may be me," Rosa says with a sigh.

"I think you are right. If Paul takes you to put in place in the future, your mom and dad have no offspring because Helen was gone. What the heck is this?" Alice grinds out.

They both are at a loss for words. Suddenly, Rosa covers her face with her hands and begins to cry. Alice places her hand on Rosa's shoulder and pats her on the shoulder.

"Rosa, the summer break is just around the corner. How about going somewhere for a rest. I'm gonna ask my mom if we can stay in her summer house. Let them do their jobs and you'd better stay out of them," Alice says.

Rosa stops crying and says, "Thanks, you are thoughtful."

9

Two colorful birds are singing on a fig tree which has grown tall enough to cover the window of Nancy's room. The birds always fly to the windowsill from its branches. Inside the window two guinea pigs pay no attention to the birds at all. In the luxury cage placed close to the window they are moving here and there to eat or to play together in their big cage. These guinea pigs moved in relatively recently when Paul presented them to Nancy as a gift.

Nancy wasn't pleased with them at first but soon began to open her mind to them. She stared at them for hours and then shared affection with them when naming them after her late children. As she watched them moving minute by minute all day long, she could feel better and better. She seemed to find her own way of coping with her children's death even though she may never get over her loss.

Eventually she opens her laptop and continues writing her everyday life which has been stopped for two years. The past two years have been hell for her missing her late two kids and feeling tremendous guilt. While Nancy has been preoccupied with her own thoughts, the door is opened.

"Nancy, I knocked the door several times, but there's no answer. So I opened it without your permission," Paul says at the door.

"It's okay. Come on in, dad. What's up?" Nancy says without looking at him.

Paul seems to be surprised by her reaction because she hasn't responded to anybody so far.

"You look great. What a nice day! Well, I'd be happy if you make time for me," Paul says.

"Oh. Do you have anything to tell me? Well, talk to

me now," Nancy says.

"It's trivial stuff. Hmm, forget it. I think your mom and I can take care of it. Well, how about playing golf next week?" Paul asks reading her face.

"That sounds good. I'm available any time, you know," Nancy says with a smile.

Paul wonders if she's doing fine because she's totally a different person. As soon as Paul gets out of her room, he goes to Olivia and says, "Our daughter has changed. She says she can play golf with us next week. I think she's back to her former self."

Paul and Olivia look into each other thinking how Nancy is going to react if she meets Rosa who takes Nancy's eyes and lips. Once Nancy knows Rosa as her own kid she won't miss the chance no matter what it takes. Now that Paul has requested Rosa's DNA test after meeting with Linda, he can't put things back the way they were.

10

As night falls, Linda's nerves become unstrung. She jumps out of bed and walks across the living room to the kitchen. She puts the kettle on the gas stove to make tea. Since Paul took Rosa's toothbrush for DNA test, her worries get deeper. That Anne doesn't look serious about the presence of Paul leaves Linda to shoulder a psychological burden.

Startled by the sound of kettle, she leaps to her feet. Sipping tea she goes to the living room and sits on the sofa. She grabs her cell phone checking the time to call Anne but she gives up. She sits still and mumbles, "I'd better wait till the result of DNA testing. It's up to Paul. I can't see how he will proceed. But I don't understand why he wants his biological granddaughter back after seventeen years. It's odd. There must be something wrong with him. On Helen's side she would feel betrayed if she figured it out. Does his daughter know what Paul's doing? Oh, gosh, I can't sleep!" She hears the clock strike midnight.

When she thinks of Rosa, she feels heartbroken. Rosa is a good granddaughter--positive, bright and smart--who Linda has loved so much. She wants to watch Rosa as a family member as long as she lives. At her age anything can't be a pleasure except puppies, but Rosa grows up as a meaningful pleasure for Linda. So Linda must keep Rosa around for her own sake.

All of a sudden, the cell phone rings in the middle of the night and it wakes Linda who was asleep on the sofa.

That's the call from Anne. "What's up? Oh, it's dawn," Linda presses on the cell and says.

"Yeah, I know. Rosa didn't come home without any notice. Yesterday was the last school day before the summer break. I thought she was in her room. You know, this is the first time. I kept calling her but she didn't answer it," Anne says in a quavering voice.

"Really? You'd better text her. Then she'll text you back. I'll be right there," Linda says.

"No, come here in the morning, mom. I'll call you if I have any message from Rosa. I already texted Alice to ask if she saw Rosa," Anne says.

Lying on a beach chair Rosa watches the sun rise over the lake, and fixes her gaze on the forest along the lake in the distance which glitters in the sun thinking of Anne who called her almost twenty times since dawn. This time, Rosa ignores her mom unlike how she has been. She just wants to be free from people around her and needs time to refresh herself.

Rosa hears Alice call out from the living room of the summer house and rises to her feet and says that she's coming.

"Rosa! Your mother texted me several times. Do

you think I should tell her you are here?" Alice asks.

"Oh, I'll text her we are together to study for SAT test here," Rosa answers.

Rosa begins to text her mom instead of calling, "Mom, sorry for not telling you yesterday but I didn't have time to call you. And I was asleep as soon as I had dinner here, the summer house of Alice's mother. We are gonna study together for SAT and I think we'll stay for about a week until the summer school starts. You can ask Alice's mom about our location and don't worry about us. We are safe here. You know, I'm a fast runner as well as a black belt in judo, so I can knock out strangers. I'll text you every hour. I love you."

"I'm done. Let's hit the road to the nearby restaurant. I'll buy you breakfast," Rosa grins.

"Don't. We have a lot of stuff in the fridge. I'll make omelet for us. How about that?" Alice asks.
They both wash their hands and begin to peel onions. Rosa looks relaxed forgetting Paul and seems to feel good.

During their stay there they swim in the lake as often as they want and read books on the beach chairs. When they study SAT Roy join them at Alice's request. Since Alice knows that Rosa has a crush on Roy, she invites him to make Rosa feel happy with his presence. He also never comes to them empty handed. Instead, he fills his backpack with some goodies and interesting stuff like a puzzle toy.

A week has passed in a flash since Rosa and Alice stayed in the summer house. Rosa loved spending her time jogging around the lake. On the day Rosa plans to go back home she receives a text message on her cell phone. It reads "Hi, sweetheart! What time are you coming home? Text me when you leave."

Rosa wears her sneakers to jog one more time before leaving the lake and says to Alice that she'll be back in an hour. She steps into the winding path around the lake to run. Though the path is deserted, she is safe in broad daylight because she has never seen any animals while jogging. She runs as usual but a bit faster feeling something behind her and stops completely at a cougar which shows up in a flash. And suddenly, it collapses before attacking her. She is breathless in an unspeakable moment, and hears a man's voice. She looks back to find out what's happening behind her. To her surprise, there stands a man in his mid thirties.

"Oh my god, did you kill it?" Rosa asks with a look of shock.

"No, I shot it some anesthetic. It almost bit you. What the hell are you doing without safety equipment?" the man glares at Rosa.

"It's the first time to see this thing. Thank you so much, Mister. By the way you run faster than I do. I didn't see anyone when I started jogging," Rosa says.

"You're welcome. I think you'd better go back to your place. I should call 911 to take this one," the man says.

Rosa runs back the way she ran after appreciating his help one more time.

Sitting in the passenger seat of Alice's car, Rosa thinks of the man who saved her from a cougar. Without his help, Rosa would be in danger. It seemed to be an odd coincidence that appeared at the pertinent timing because Rosa didn't see anyone behind her while running. Rosa is curious about the man and even regrets not asking his name, never expecting that Paul has hired a bodyguard for her safety.

Being welcomed by Anne, Rosa goes upstairs to her room and unpacks her bag. She makes up her mind not to think about her future no matter what happens but to focus on doing her job to get into an Ivy League college a year later. Getting away for a week has a restful effect on Rosa.

11

Paul and Olivia have seated in a restaurant waiting for Nancy, their daughter. They have never dreamed of having dinner in the restaurant for almost two years since Nancy lost her kids in a car accident. While waiting, Olivia checks if she has an envelope in her purse that gives the result of DNA testing on Rosa that matches that of Nancy.

"Sorry, I took the wrong way," Nancy says and sits on the chair across from them.

They order what they want from a menu. In the middle of dinner Nancy looks over her parents' faces and says, "You both look good. I guess you have good news for me."

"I'll tell you after finishing my meal," Paul says with a smile.

As Olivia finishes her meal, she takes out a piece of paper from the envelope and put it on the table. She takes a deep breath and says to Nancy, "Read this one."

"Well, let's see. Rosa's DNA matches mine. What? Oh my god! You mean Helen isn't mine? Who is Rosa?" Nancy asks with a shock.

Paul starts to tell the long story that has happened so far and finishes with saying that Miller's family doesn't know the result. After hearing every word Paul said, Nancy seems to be speechless.

"I don't know what to tell you, dad. I can't believe this paper," Nancy mumbles.

Paul continues, "I'm going to take her back to you. She's your real daughter. It took almost two years for me to find her."

"Wait a minute. What? Are you planning to take Rosa away from her family? She's a teen, not a baby. Don't tell them the result, please. No!" Nancy says and holds her head in her hands.

They skip dessert and leave to go back home.

Paul and Olivia get to the house before Nancy and then hear the garage door shut. Night falls, but Nancy can't fall asleep. Lying on the bed she stares at the ceiling vacantly and thinks of Helen who was a beautiful girl with a fair complexion and cobalt-blue eyes. Nancy was used to hear from people around her that Helen didn't take after her at all. Nancy didn't care about that saying Helen might take after her great-grandmother. As of now, Helen's absence is making Nancy feel empty and lonely, but she becomes curious about Rosa as she hears the clock ticking. Paul told Nancy that Rosa looks just like Nancy: brown eyes, curly brunette hair, healthy complexion and an athletic. Nancy sits up and begins to check her cell phone records. Thankfully, she finds a message from Roy.

Nancy texts Roy. "Hi, this is Nancy, Helen's mom. I'm sorry to bother you so late. I'm just wondering if you know Rosa who goes to the same school. Can I ask you a favor? Will you tell Rosa that a woman wants to see her at the school library tomorrow at noon?"

Nancy receives an answer from Roy. "Hi, I'm so glad to hear from you, Mrs. Greene. I'll do that for you. You don't want me to mention your name to her, do you? All right. I'll let you know if Rosa can meet tomorrow morning."

Nancy texts, "Thanks, I appreciate your help. You're very thoughtful. Good night."

In the morning Nancy gets a message from Roy that Rosa will show up at the library at noon. Nancy has fixed her eyes on the clock of the kitchen to check the time all morning before leaving home. She arrives at the school parking lot five minutes ahead of time and goes right to the library. Stepping into the hall, she puts on her sunglasses and finds Rosa first who is standing at the library door.

At first sight, Nancy is struck by Rosa's face which

is definitely taking after Nancy. Like Paul said Rosa looks exactly the same as Nancy does. Holding her excitement Nancy tries to calm down and passes Rosa as if she is a passerby. Nancy feels Rosa cast a glance at Nancy. Just to be sure, Rosa is staring at Nancy who goes to the end of the hall and disappears to the door on the right. Rosa looks like she doesn't know who is going to be her visitor.

In the room where Nancy walks in mindlessly, a woman sits at the desk looks up at Nancy in surprise.

Nancy is at a loss. "Woops, I was looking for the library door, ma'am. I'm sorry to interrupt you here at work." She continues to talk about personal things to buy some time. A woman at the desk kindly asks Nancy whose mother she is. At that moment Nancy excuses herself and gets out of the room.

In the hallway Nancy finds no one at the library door and begins to feel forlorn. She keeps looking around while heading to the entrance of the building. In her mind Nancy wants Rosa back right away to fill a big hole in her heart which was formed after Helen died. On the way home Nancy stops by Paul and Olivia who are at work together. Nancy knows they have been always on her side and ready to do everything for her.

"Hey, guys. Can you guess what I did? I saw Rosa. Last night, I asked Roy to arrange a meeting with her without telling who's coming to see her. Oh, at first glance she was my daughter. I could see she knew nothing. She'll never expect what's going on around her. Poor Rosa! She'll get hurt if she finds out our existence," Nancy says with a confused look on her face.

"If Helen was here with me, I would have never wanted Rosa back no matter what happened. Though Helen didn't take after me at all, she was my loving girl." A sad smile comes over her face.

"Dad, you didn't tell Linda the result of DNA testing yet, did you? I think we need time to think it over. And, don't even think about a suit or something."

"Okay, Nancy. I'll wait. But I think we should take

Rosa back as an heir. I mean we have no offspring but you," Paul says.

Nancy shrugs her shoulders. "But it's not that simple. If Helen had been alive, Rosa wouldn't have been in my life. If we get Rosa back, the Millers should have Helen, but it's impossible. Oh, it's all my fault. I miss poor Helen!" Nancy begins to sob. Olivia draws Nancy close to her and lays her hand on Nancy's shoulder looking at Paul.

"Oh, sweetie, we're gonna try to make everything good," Olivia says softly.

12

When Rosa comes home from school, she sees Linda's dog playing in the driveway. As Rosa approaches the garage, it glances at Rosa and moves to another bush sniffing. In the kitchen Linda is chopping the tomato to make the casserole. She seems to focus on cooking without noticing Rosa coming.

"Hi, grandma, I'm home. Hmm, you're making a good dish. You always please my nose," Rosa says.

"Oh, I didn't hear you come in. Nora didn't bark at you, huh. How was your school?" Linda says.

"Good, by the way I didn't make it when I was supposed to meet a woman at the library door. It was a favor for Roy. But she didn't show up."

"Roy? Who is he? I haven't heard of him," Linda says.

"He's Alice's friend. This morning he told me a woman wanted to see me at noon. I have no idea who she is," Rosa says taking her cell phone.

"Hmm. I wonder who she is, too. But forget it," Linda says thinking of Olivia.

Linda is sure of Paul getting the result of DNA testing.

Under the hot sun things go well as if nothing has happened. Rosa studies hard to get excellent grades and her family members do their work as usual. Linda only spends her days with her heart in her mouth because she is anxious about how Paul will do the action with the proof of DNA. Every morning she checks the mailbox on arriving at Anne's house and then does her daily job which Anne has never asked.

By the time Linda gets tired of watching her cell phone to check whether she has received any message from the Parkers, she hears the phone ringing in the living room. She is startled at the sound and then almost fainted at the news of Rosa's hospitalization after she ran her bike into a car. Automatically she calls Olivia to let her know what happened to Rosa. And then she makes a face and tilts her head thinking it's ridiculous that Olivia was the first person to be called regarding Rosa instead of Anne.

Linda rushes to the hospital to see Rosa. In the emergency room, Paul and Olivia stand at the foot of the bed, looking at Rosa with serious faces. When Linda approaches, she sees a woman beside Olivia who looks just like Rosa.

"Oh my gosh, she looks like Rosa. I should call Anne not to come now," Linda mutters to herself.

Rosa seems to sleep after being treated with a shot. Luckily enough, she has a bruise on her left thigh and a sprained wrist. The Parkers feel gratitude for Rosa's surviving the accident.

"Thanks, Lord! She's not that bad. I was so shocked when I got the phone call from the hospital. How are you doing?" Linda says.

"We are fine, thanks. It's still summer, huh. We've had a tough time, I guess. I don't know what to say, but we should have time together," Paul says.

"Well, this is Nancy, our daughter."

"Nancy, this is Ms. Linda Stewart, Rosa's grandmother."

Nancy smiles at Linda and says, "Nice to meet you, Ms. Stewart. I heard much of you from my father."

"Oh, I see. Well, how are things going? I've been waiting for your call, Paul," Linda says.

"Yeah, I suppose so. I wanted to call you, but Nancy kept me from doing that. I think we need to make some time to discuss after Rosa gets well," Paul says with a smile.

While they are talking a little, Rosa has been awake with her eyes closed guessing Nancy is late Helen's mother. She knows that the discussion is meant to be her DNA stuff, and Linda may be nervous about what they will do in the near future. It's up to Nancy to decide whether they will take Rosa from Miller's family. She easily can imagine how her poor grandmother, Linda, looks in front of them. But she pretends sleeping as an innocent girl.

About the time when Rosa's cast is off, Linda visits Paul's house on his request. She pulls herself together at the front door before ringing the doorbell. Nancy welcomes Linda with a sweet smile and leads her to the reception room. At a glance, she sees that the room is luxuriously furnished. Sitting on a sky blue leather sofa Linda looks around every corner of the room. "Every piece of furniture looks posh. I love to see antique furniture."

"Thank you, Linda. We collect things whenever we travel and especially, Nancy loves to buy high end products," Olivia says looking at Nancy.

"Oh, I think Nancy has excellent taste. Well, then, let's get to the point. I think Rosa's DNA matches that of Nancy. If so, I wonder what's on your mind. I mean what's your next move?" Linda says.

Paul gives Linda a concerned look before he starts to say. "Well. As you know, Rosa's DNA tells that she's Nancy's daughter. But we can't make any decision right now. Linda, there's a story I didn't tell you yet. Well, I don't know if you would forgive us. Um….there was a horrible accident two years ago," Paul says.

He continues, "Up to two years ago, Nancy lived well with Helen and Tom, her son, though she was divorced. But Nancy had a car accident that turned her life into a living hell. She lost Helen and Tom in a week after the accident. We had all been devastated by the sad tragic incident. One day while we were in a living hell, I found a piece of paper. It showed that Helen's blood type was B. So I was shocked because it couldn't be done. Both Nancy and her ex-husband were A. So, I recalled the day when I met you in the hospital and set out to find you to confirm Rosa is related to us by blood. Of course, we still love Helen so much. If we didn't lose Helen, we would have no chance to see you.

Honestly, I'm very sorry to say like this, but we need an heir after Nancy. I hope you understand me."

As Paul finishes his talking, he sees Linda's face become distorted. But soon she seems to regain composure.

"Well, first of all, I'm so sorry for your loss. Speaking of the newborn unit, I have been agonizing about what I was supposed to do seventeen years ago since you appeared in front of me. I know it wasn't my fault about the ID bands because I didn't do anything about it at that moment. But now I'm only thinking of my daughter, Anne. She can't think of this. She can't live without Rosa. Besides, now that Helen's gone, how can I persuade Anne to let Rosa go to your family? Paul, what can I say to her? If you take Rosa away from Anne without Helen, you are destroying her family," Linda says.

"You're absolutely right. I won't let Anne go through what I've suffered from. So we are considering our next move carefully. Ms. Stewart, I'm so sorry about Helen. I still love her so much," Nancy says with tears in her eyes.

"Linda, I completely understand how you feel. But I don't think I can leave it as it is. Do you mind if I meet your son-in-law to talk about this? I'll have a man-to-man talk," Paul says, interrupting Nancy,

"Brian? Well, yeah. That's an idea. He'll be shocked at first, but he may handle this problem rationally. I'll set the time for you. Are you gonna see him alone?" Linda says.

"No. I think you should come and I'll take Nancy since she's involved in this matter. Thank you so much for your cooperation. And once again we feel so sorry for this whole situation. You're very thoughtful," Paul says.

13

On the way home Linda watches the trees pass by the window and finds some leaves are turning red. Since Paul appeared to Linda, every day has been like walking on eggshells. So she never feels how the summer goes by. All she can think of is how to keep Rosa in Anne's family because no one else replaces Rosa.

She pulls her car in the garage and texts her son-in-law, "Brian, I want you to meet me alone sometime soon. Please let me know when you are available."

A few minutes later a message from Brian pops up. It reads, "I can see you tomorrow in the afternoon."

In a cafeteria where only one table is occupied by a

lady, Linda takes a seat looking around to find Brian. She sees Paul and Nancy get inside and Brian after them. Linda waves her hand to them and they all sit at the table.

"Hello, my name is Paul Parker and this is Nancy, my daughter. I really appreciate your being here to talk," Paul says.

"Hello, I'm Brian Miller. I'm wondering what we're here for. Linda wants to see me, so I didn't expect anyone. Anyway I guess there's a serious matter to discuss," Brian says.

Then Brian pays attention to Nancy because she looks like Rosa, but he ignores what he sees. When Paul begins to explain why he and Nancy would like to see Brian, Brian listens to Paul cautiously. As the story that Paul tells reaches what he has done for two years, Brian's face becomes grave.

Meanwhile, Nancy recognizes Brian at a glance and sits quite still dropping her eyes to avoid eye contact with Brian. In fact, Brian hasn't been involved in her life. He didn't go to the same college with her nor worked with her. He is the man who Nancy just met once by chance. She recalls the night of eighteen years ago. Brian was on a business trip when he joined Nancy at the bar by accident. At that night Nancy was extremely depressed by her husband who had cheated on her, and she had beer more than she should have. She remembers that they talked a lot, especially Nancy shared her unhappy marriage with him, but they both drank too much and Nancy blacked out. At dawn Nancy woke up at a hotel and she found Brian sleeping on the other bed in a twin room. She left the room quickly feeling embarrassed.

Up to this afternoon Nancy has never thought of Brian and even doesn't know his name. Glancing at Brian Nancy tries to calm herself down feeling grateful for his presence as Rosa's father and mumbles, "What a coincidence to see him like this!"

Brian with a serious look stares at the floor when Paul finishes his talking and he is silent for a few minutes. He seems to be shocked since he wasn't given any information by Linda.

"Mr. Parker, first of all, I'm so sorry for your loss. But I don't know what to say about such a bizarre story. I can't believe what I'm hearing. Hmm. This is absurd and how can we fix this situation? If I hear you properly, in a nutshell, you want Rosa back because you lost Helen and Rosa's DNA matches to that of Nancy. So, you plan to file a paternity suit based on Rosa's DNA, if we don't agree with you." Brian's face flushes red with anger.

"Mr. Miller, I didn't say it, right now. And Nancy wouldn't dare want Rosa in her family. I'd like to say that we apologize for bringing up this complicated issue. You must be confused and angry," Paul says.

"And it's hard for us to talk about late Helen. We still love her too much and miss her everyday."
Brian doesn't respond to Paul and takes a deep breath. Suddenly, Nancy's face jumps to the eyes so that Brian stares at Nancy to figure out if she is an acquaintance.

In a minute the conviction flashes across his mind that Nancy is just the woman Brian talked with through the night about eighteen years ago. Brian mumbles to himself, "Oh, boy! She gave birth to Rosa after that night. By the way, she really looks like Rosa. If Anne knows this, she's gonna be freaked out." Then Brian is wondering what if Rosa has his DNA. He shakes head thinking it's not likely because nothing happened that night. But he decides to keep Rosa as his daughter no matter what Paul does insisting on DNA stuff.

"Then, Mr. Parker, did you ask the DNA testing agency to examine whether Rosa's DNA matches to Nancy's husband?" Brian asks.

At this point Nancy looks at Brian in the eyes and takes his suggestion with a pinch of salt. And she says, "Dad, I think he sounds right. We need to ask the agency to examine Kevin's DNA. And then we'd better discuss it further. Thank you so much, both of you, I hope we will find the best way to get along together."

It takes a month to find Kevin, and Nancy asks him for DNA testing. The result comes out a week later that Rosa is exactly Nancy and Kevin's biological daughter. The result seems to disappoint Nancy a bit who expected a slim chance, but it feels like she finished a big assignment since she didn't mean to hurt Miller's family from the beginning.

Nancy brings Olivia and Paul together in Paul's study.

"Mom, Dad, Rosa is Kevin's child. But, you know what? Brian isn't a stranger. I met Brian eighteen years ago and we spent one night together--both drunk and nothing happened. Funny enough, I wished to tell you Brian is Rosa's father. I know you may think I'm crazy." Nancy shrugs her shoulders.

"We understand you. You say Brian has nothing to do with Rosa. But he isn't Mr. nobody to you, right? That's a big surprise. Anyway, but I'm glad to hear that news. I bet you made up your mind, right? We'll do whatever you say, Nancy," Paul says.

"Yes, I made up my mind. Brian isn't related with Rosa at all, but it's not that bad if he lives with her. And I really don't want to hurt Anne. If she knows her real daughter doesn't exist on earth, she'll go crazy without Rosa. I can't do that bad thing to her. If we tell the truth to Anne when we get Rosa back, she won't let it go as we wish. I hope all's well. So I want you both to tell Linda that nothing changes and we'll stay as close friends. If you want an heir, you can make your money be placed in a trust fund for Rosa. Oh, dad, do me a favor. Don't look at Rosa like you're her grandpa, please. You both can't help loving your only granddaughter, though," Nancy says.

Paul and Olivia nod their heads at the same time agreeing with Nancy, and Paul says,

"You're very thoughtful, hmm. Okay, we will stay as family friends. Well, fall is just around the corner. It means your mom's birthday is coming up soon. I'll throw a big birthday party for you, Olivia. We'll get together with the Millers and Linda."

"That's a great idea. I'll let Brian know what we talked about. And I hope Anne and Brian accept me as their friend. Oh, I'm so happy," Nancy says with a big smile.

14

One morning in mid-September when Rosa pulls her bike in the garage to go to school, she finds a red brand new sedan in the drive way.

"Dad, did you buy a new car?" Rosa calls out Brian.

"No, it's yours! It's a surprise gift for you," Brian says approaching Rosa.

"What? Oh, you bought it in secret!" Anne runs out of the kitchen.

"What a nice car! I'm happy for you, Rosa. You know how to drive, right?" Anne says.

"Sure! mom. But today's not my birthday, huh. Dad, is your business going well?" Rosa says and kisses on Brian's cheek.

"Thank you so much, daddy. I have to leave now. I'll talk to you guys later," Rosa says getting on her bike without knowing that gift is from Paul.

One October evening, Rosa gets into her red sedan and sits in the driver's seat. While waiting for her parents and Linda to go together to Paul's house to attend Olivia's birthday party, she looks up at the sky and trees feeling a crisp, gold-tinged autumn. Since she decided to focus on her study, she hasn't minded what Paul and Olivia were doing with Linda. And now she understands the whole thing--being chased by her real grandparents who tried to get her to listen to them and DNA issue and Nancy who watched her at the library and giving up the process to take her away from Anne and becoming family friends with the Millers. The night when she was freaked at the subway station remains one of the memorable incidents in her life. She smiles at herself by feeling proud to be a sweet innocent girl.

In a few minutes, Linda, Brian and Anne come to

the car.

"Welcome to my Ancyiadapauli, three blond guys," Rosa shouts happily.

"Who is Ancyiadapauli?" Anne asks as soon as she sits in the back seat of the car.

"It's my car. I named it. Let's go, my Ancyiadapauli," Rosa says with a smile and starts the car.

Rosa sees Linda wink at her in the rearview mirror.